DATE DUE

DEC. 16			
JAN. 21			
JAN. 29			
MAR. 17			
OCT. 20			
			Printed in USA

WITHDRAWN

HIGHSMITH #45230

Getting Ready

A Career as a Video Game Designer

by Bill Lund

Content Consultant:
Rik Sandoval, Director
Computer Game Developers Association

CAPSTONE PRESS
MANKATO, MINNESOTA

C A P S T O N E   P R E S S

818 North Willow Street • Mankato, Minnesota 56001
http://www.capstone-press.com

Printed in the United States of America.

Library of Congress Cataloging-in-Publication Data
    Lund, Bill, 1954-
    Getting ready for a career as a video game designer/by Bill Lund.
    p. cm.
    Includes bibliographical references and index.
    Summary: Discusses the development of video games as well as the skills
    and education required for a career as a game designer.
    ISBN 1-56065-552-6
    1. Computer games--Programming--Vocational guidance--Juvenile
literature. 2. Video games--Design--Vocational guidance--Juvenile literature.
[1. Video games--Design--Vocational guidance.   2. Electronic games--
Vocational guidance. 3. Vocational guidance.]
I. Title.
QA76.76.C672L86   1998
794.8'151--dc21

                              97-9397
                               CIP
                               AC

Photo Credits
FPG/Ed Taylor Studio, 14; Ron Chapple, 18; Jim McNee, 22; Reggie Parker,
   24; Arthur Tilley, 29; Navaswan, 30
Nintendo of America, 21, 37
Silicon Graphics, cover
Unicorn Stock/James L. Fly, 4; Jim Shippee, 7, 28; Bill McMackins, 9; Eric
   R. Berndt, 10, 13, 33; Shellie Nelson, 15; Karen Helsinger Mullen, 16;
   Florent Flipper, 17; Remi, 26; Tom McCarthy, 34; Tom and DeeAnn
   McCarthy, 36; Martin R. Jones, 39; Tommy Dodson, 42; Jeff Greenberg,
   45; Herbert L. Stormont, 47

Table of Contents

SONIC CD™

GAME 5 MINUTES

SCORE 0
TIME 0'09"61
RINGS 3

SEGA CDX™

Chapter 1
A Career in Video Games

Almost everyone has played a video game at least once. A video game is an electronic or computerized game. Some video games are Nintendo's *Super Mario Bros.*® and Sega's *Sonic the Hedgehog*®. People play some games at home and some in video arcades. An arcade is a place with many games that people pay to play. Handheld video games allow video game players to play just about anywhere.

Creating video games is a multi-billion dollar business. People in North America spend

Some people play video games in arcades.

$5 billion a year on video games. Video game designers create video games.

Designers and Teams

Video game designers think of new ideas and plan new games. Sometimes they make games by themselves. Usually video game designers lead design teams in making games. The members of a team are trained in certain areas.

Design teams include people who write stories, make music, draw pictures, and program software. Program means to enter a set of instructions to make a computer work a certain way. Software is a set of programs that tells a computer what to do. A program is a set of instructions that makes a computer work a certain way. Designers work together to create games.

Many people work for a long time to create video games. Twenty-eight people created Nintendo's *Donkey Kong Country*™. A design team may take months or years to create a game.

Success and Failure

The video game business produces many video games each year. Manufacturers made more than 4,000 different games in 1996. At a 1997 video game convention, designers introduced 1,500 new games. A convention is a gathering of people with similar interests.

The video game business produces many new video games each year.

Not all games are successes. A game may be too hard to play or not hard enough. Some players may not like a game's pictures or music. Some games might be too expensive. People might not buy these games.

But some video games succeed. They are challenging but fun to play. Many people buy them. Between 1985 and 1987, people bought a million copies of Nintendo's *The Legend of Zelda*®.

Video game businesses need designers to make their new games. More than 90,000 people work in the video game business. The number of people working in the business is increasing by 26 percent each year. This means there are many jobs for new video game designers.

People enjoy challenging and fun video games.

Chapter 2
Video Game Advancement

Video games are a new addition to the world of games. They were created around 30 years ago. Video games and video game machines have changed a lot since then.

The History of Video Games

Steve Russell created the first video game in 1962. He was a college student. He made a game called *Spacewar*. It was a simple game. Little space ships flew through a starry sky. The object of the game was to shoot an enemy's ship out of the sky.

Video games and video game machines have changed a lot in the past 30 years.

People played *Spacewar* on computers. But not everyone had computers. *Spacewar* players wanted everyone to play the game.

Nolan Bushnell was an inventor. He played *Spacewar* in college. He decided to put video games in arcades.

In 1972, Bushnell put the first video game in an arcade. It was a game like *Spacewar* called *Computer Space*. *Computer Space* was hard to play. People did not like it.

Bushnell created an American company called Atari to create a new game. Atari made *Pong*, an electronic table tennis game. Atari put *Pong* in arcades. The game was a huge success because it was easy to play but challenging. Many people liked to play it.

Soon, more companies entered the video game business. By 1982, video games were popular. Video game designers created two famous games that year. One was *Pac-Man*®. Players of this game move a character named Pac-Man through mazes. The mazes are filled with dots and ghosts. Players make Pac-Man eat the dots and avoid the ghosts.

Nintendo's *Donkey Kong*® was another famous game. In *Donkey Kong*, players help Mario avoid barrels and boards thrown by a gorilla. Mario is a little man with a red hat.

Video game players liked the Mario character. Video game designers decided to make him the main character of a game. In 1985, designers created *Super Mario Bros.*

Players of *Pac-Man* move Pac-Man through mazes filled with dots and ghosts.

The Progress of Game Machines

People enjoy video games on several types of machines. Video games in arcades are stored on computers inside large, upright consoles. A console is a cabinet that stands on the floor. People play the games with joysticks. A joystick is a handle that controls movement in a video game. Buttons on the machine also control movements.

People play games on personal computers.

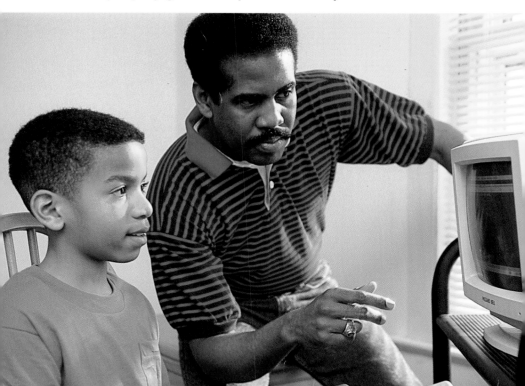

Many people own video game systems.

People also play video games in their homes. They play games on video game systems. A video game system is a small computer that is connected to a television. In the United States, 45 percent of families own video game systems. People play games on personal computers, too. A personal computer is a computer used by a single person or family.

Some video games are stored on CD-ROMs.

Manufacturers store home video games in different ways. They store games on floppy disks, CD-ROMs, or game cartridges. A disk is film housed inside a plastic casing. A CD-ROM is a compact disk that stores information such as video game software. CD-ROM stands for compact disk read only

16

memory. A game cartridge is a plastic casing that stores video game software. A cartridge is put in a video game system.

People also play video games on handheld video game machines. These machines are small enough to fit in a pocket. Some are the size of a wristwatch.

People play video games on handheld video game machines.

Chapter 3
Designing a Video Game

Video game designers perform many tasks. They write storylines and program software. A storyline is a series of events in a story. Designers make music and create graphics. Graphics are the pictures in a video game.

Video game designers might perform these tasks alone. Sometimes a team comes together to create a game. Members of a team specialize in each part of creating a game. Specialize means to train in one area of work or to study one subject.

Video game designers work as a team to create video games.

All video games start as ideas. Video game designers think of new characters. They invent worlds for characters. Designers create goals for games. They create problems for game characters. They must think of rules for games. Video game designers must carefully plan out their new ideas.

Writing the Storyline

Video games have storylines that go with the action. Players move characters through storylines as they play games. In *Super Mario Bros.*, players move Mario through several worlds as he tries to rescue a princess. With each new storyline, designers think of new adventures for video game characters.

Video game designers write storylines. They decide where games will start. They decide how players will advance in games. Then they put storylines on storyboards. A storyboard is an outline for a video game.

Designing Graphics

Video game designers decide how video games will look. Designers must have artistic talent and understand computers well. Sometimes graphic designers help game designers create the appearance of a game. A graphic designer is a person who creates pictures for games, computers, books, or magazines.

Video game designers use computer animation to create characters and backgrounds

In Nintendo's *Super Mario 64*™, Mario tries to rescue a princess.

that move. Computer animation is a way of drawing pictures so they seem to move.

Scores and instructions often appear in video games. Video game designers choose the sizes, shapes, and colors of letters that appear in games.

Creating Sound Effects

Video game designers invent sound effects for games. A sound effect is a sound that

Video game designers program software.

accompanies a video game. Sometimes audio engineers help designers make sounds for games. An audio engineer is a person who creates and designs sound effects.

The first video games had simple sounds. *Pong* made beeping noises each time players hit the ball. *Pac-Man* made a series of beeps as Pac-Man ate dots. A simple song played when the game started and when a player finished a maze.

Today, video games have many sound effects. Sounds accompany most movements of game characters. Songs play during games. Sometimes voices explain instructions to game players.

Video game designers record music, sounds, and voices that accompany video games. They also change sounds. They make sounds higher, lower, faster, or slower. They even add echos.

Programming Software

Video game designers program game software. Game software is a set of programs that a computer uses to run a video game. Designers

must know programming codes. A programming code is a language that a computer will understand.

New games often have mistakes in their programs. For example, a computer might not understand part of a code. Or the code might be wrong. Mistakes in a program are called bugs. Designers work to fix the bugs. This is called debugging. Debugging game programs is not easy. Sometimes it takes designers weeks or months to debug programs.

A finished video game combines music, sound effects, and animated graphics. The storyline and the rules of the game make it fun or educational. Programming brings the parts together to create a video game.

Debugging game programs may take designers weeks or months.

Chapter 4
Career Preparation

Playing video games can be fun. Video game designers should enjoy playing video games. But designing video games is a career with many challenges. People who want to design games must have certain skills. They have to attend school to learn about science, math, art, music, writing, and computers.

Skills

Video game designers work with computers. They use computers to design different parts of games. Designers must be comfortable working with computers.

Video game designers attend school to learn about science, math, art, music, writing, and computers.

27

Video game designers are creative. They think of new ideas for games. Designers think of fun characters. Each character looks and acts differently. Designers think of fun adventures, too. Every game has new problems to solve and new worlds to explore.

Video game designers also need other skills. They should be good writers because they write storylines. They should be able to draw

Every game has new problems to solve and new worlds to explore.

Video game designers have to work together and be patient.

since they design game characters. They should know a lot about music so they can think of new songs and sounds for games.

If they work with a team, video game designers must be able to share ideas and problems. Designers have to work together and be patient. Games will not turn out well if team members do not get along.

Education and Training

All video game designers should attend high school. Designers need to know about math and science to program computers. Studying math and science in high school gives them strong backgrounds. Learning about computers is important. Students will be ready to learn harder skills if they understand basic skills. Designers also should learn about art, writing, and music in high school.

Some video game designers go to technical college.

Some video game designers go to technical colleges for two years. A technical college offers classes that include hands-on training for certain jobs. Students can learn programming codes at technical colleges. Designers must know codes to tell computers what to do. They may also learn about computer programs or design.

Other video game designers go to college for four years. They earn degrees in computer science, design, writing, or music. A degree is a title given by a college or university for completing a course of study. Some earn degrees in video game design. These designers have classes in computer animation, programming, game ideas, and storyboards.

Many people learn about game design by helping other game designers. After they attend school, they may start working as assistants. Other designers help them train and learn more about video game design. Later, they may work as designers.

Starting Early

People who want to be video game designers can start early. They should play video games often. They should try many different games. Then they will know how different games work. They may develop ideas for new games if they know about other games.

Some video game companies have game testers. Testers must like to play games because they test games all day. Testers play new games to find out if the games are good. If testers enjoy the games, other people will probably enjoy them, too.

Testers also look for problems or bugs in games. Sometimes graphics might not look life-like. Certain commands might not work. Testers tell video game designers about problems. Some testers become designers.

People who want to be video game designers should play video games often.

Chapter 5
The Future of Video Games

Video games are becoming more popular every year. The first games were simple. Now games have many parts. They are harder to design. Making new and challenging games is important in the video game business.

New Games
Many people have personal computers in their homes. Some video game designers make games for computers. These games are stored on CD-ROMs or floppy disks. Computers can read CD-ROMs and floppy disks.

Video games are becoming more popular every year.

People now play games on their computers. They do not have to go to arcades. They do not have to buy video game systems for their televisions. But many still enjoy arcades and video game systems.

Today's games have three dimensional (3-D) graphics. Three dimensional means appearing to have length, width, and height. Video games look more life-like with 3-D graphics.

People now play games on their computers.

Video games now have 3-D graphics.

Early games each had one ending. Some games today have many endings. These games are interactive. In an interactive game, players make choices to control and change the result of a game. Players' choices are acted out by characters in these games. Players choose where to go and what to do. Each choice leads to a different result.

In a game called *Myst*®, players begin the game on a dock. They can see the ocean and a ship. Players move through the scenes, but never receive any instructions. Players must choose where they will go and what they will do. Sometimes the game never ends.

Interactive games are hard to plan and program. Players have many actions from which to choose. Each choice requires separate programming.

A High-Scoring Future

Video games create exciting worlds full of challenges. Creating video games can be an exciting career. People who enjoy video games and computers may be future video game designers. They must work hard and prepare for the future.

There are many new jobs in video game design. The number of jobs is increasing every year. The video game business is growing as fast as a video game score.

People who enjoy video games and computers may be future video game designers.

Words to Know

arcade (ar-KADE)—a place with many games that people pay to play

CD-ROM (SEE DEE ROM)—a compact disk that stores pictures, words, and games; it is read by a computer.

computer animation (kuhm-PYOO-tur an-i-MAY-shuhn)—a way of drawing pictures so they seem to move

console (KON-sole)—a cabinet that stands on the floor and holds a video game

debug (dee-BUHG)—to remove mistakes in a computer program

game cartridge (GAME KAR-trij)—a plastic casing that stores video game software

graphic designer (GRAF-ik dee-ZINE-ur)—a person who creates pictures for games, computers, books, and magazines

graphics (GRAF-iks)—pictures such as drawings or maps

interactive game (in-tur-AK-tiv GAME)—a game in which players make choices to control and change the result of the game

joystick (JOI-stik)—a handle that controls movements in a video game

program (PROH-gram)—to enter instructions into a computer that make it work a certain way

software (SAWFT-wair)—a set of programs that tells a computer what to do

sound effect (SOUND uh-FEKT)—a sound that accompanies a video game

storyboard (STOR-ee-bord)—an outline for a video game

storyline (STOR-ee-line)—a series of events in a story or video game

technical college (TEK-nuh-kuhl KOL-ij)—a school that offers classes that include hands-on training for certain jobs

three dimensional (THREE duh-MEN-shuhn-uhl)—appearing to have length, width, and height

video game (VID-ee-oh GAME)—an electronic or computerized game

To Learn More

Anderson, Carol D. and Robert Sheely. *Techno Labs: How Science is Changing*. Science Labs. New York: Silver Moon Press, 1995.

Erlbach, Arlene. *Video Games*. Minneapolis: Lerner Publications, 1995.

Skurzynski, Gloria. *Know the Score: Video Games in Your High-Tech World*. New York: Bradbury Press, 1994.

Weigant, Chris. *Choosing a Career in Computers*. The World of Work. New York: Rosen Publishing Groups, 1997.

Video game designers should feel comfortable with computers.

Useful Addresses

Computer Game Developers Association
960 North San Antonio, Suite 125
Los Altos, CA 94022

DigiPen Applied Computer Graphics School
5th Floor, 530 Hornby Street
Vancouver, BC
V6C 2E7
Canada

Full Sail
3300 University Blvd.
Winter Park, FL 32792-7429

Sega of America
P.O. Box 8097
Redwood, CA 94063

In an interactive game, players make choices to
control and change the result of a game.

Internet Sites

All About Video Games
http://www1.minn.net/~schubert/VGall.html

Computer Game Developers Association
http://www.cgda.org

Nintendo
http://www.nintendo.com

The History of Home Video Games
http://www.sponsor.net/~gchance/

The video game business is growing as fast as a video game score.

Index